Sophie's Shell

Among other curious tales

Tessy Braun

Copyright © 2024 Tessy Braun

All rights reserved.

This book or any portion thereof may not be reproduced or used in any manner whatsoever without the written permission of the author, except for the use of brief quotations in a book review.

ISBN
9798879491630

DEDICATION

To my mother, Rosemary, who forever encourages my writing.

Thank you for the inspiration x

CONTENTS

Preface

Cecilia House	1
Clearwater Bay	5
The Stable Door	11
Buttered toast	19
How can I help you?	21
Sophie's Shell	31
Dig Deeper	41
Back to the Woods	51
Spin	59
About the author	**69**

PREFACE

This collection of short stories conjure up a touch of the macabre, a twist of the uncanny and a healthy portion of the shadows of times gone by.

It is my hope that the tales in this book will surprise and fright you *just* the right amount, and that they will leave you speculating about what really could be within the realms of possibility…

Tessy x

CECILIA HOUSE

My daughter asked me if I'd ever seen a ghost. I shuddered. 'Cecilia House' was *haunted as hell.* I recalled the Matron saying so after I caught a glimpse of the elderly lady in a pale blue dress on the landing.

"Dear," I sighed. "I'm a logical old duck, you know that, but yes, I've witnessed some strange things in that old house…"

I turned off the TV (the Antiques Roadshow could wait) and took the handset into the breakfast room. If we were going to 'talk ghosts', then I wanted to be in the warmest, cosiest room of my isolated old country home. I wasn't expecting my daughter's call. She's a busy mother herself, and I wondered why she had broached the subject out of the blue, especially as I knew she was travelling that day. Peter, my son, was much better at staying in touch. I could always rely on his daily telephone call.

"Old house?" Georgina asked. "You mean the nursing home you worked in for all those years?"

I nodded, even though she couldn't see me.

"That's right – *haunted as hell,* that old place was…"

"I'd love to know more. Do tell, mum."

"Alright Georgie, I will."

"Thanks mum, I wish I had called you more often. I love you."

Tessy Braun

I'll always remember the basement; cold, dank, and there was something quite unnatural about it that bothered *anyone* who had been assigned the unpleasant task of making a trip down into that big old belly of the house. I can tell you now, I'm sceptical when it comes to paranormal phenomena, and working permanent nights – well, I know very well that for many people this *can* cause fatigue, and who's to say one's perception couldn't be altered… *but* Cecilia House was strange, there was no doubt about it.

Jude, my colleague, saw shadows down in the basement; she ran out screaming one night. It was Jude who enlightened me about the history of the house and exactly what its foundations were built on. To my horror, the 1920s American style house was in fact built on the site where a gallows once stood…

It suddenly dawned on me how cold it always was in the residents' sitting room, no matter how warm the rest of the home became. It was also true, despite the abundance of chairs, there was one corner of the room where none of the residents chose to sit, claiming a draft made them feel chilly. If you ask me now, I do wonder if that cold spot was the original site of the gallows. In fact, I think it highly likely.

But what of the lady in the blue dress? Well, I saw her from the corner of my eye in the early hours. It certainly wasn't any of the residents who were all fast asleep by that time. Matron didn't have any idea as to who the lady might be, but to my complete astonishment she was not at all phased by her presence, claiming it was *obviously* one of Cecilia's many ghosts.

I might add that the Matron I speak of was a highly regarded woman of paramount intelligence and was certainly not prone to hysterical claims. I must say, it was a strange and unexpected response, though I came to learn that the atmosphere at Cecilia House was anything but normal, and to *always* expect the unexpected. From that night on, it was not uncommon for me to spot the occasional crown of a head float past the corridors while I tended to the patients (when no other staff members were known to be walking the halls at the time).

What's more, I'd frequently hear the sound of fast purposeful footsteps on the top floor corridor, but there was not one patient who wasn't bedridden at the top of the house! When I first witnessed the sound, I rushed up the stairs like there was no tomorrow, only to find the landing empty. It was *terrifying* – I'm quite sure that it couldn't be put down to vibrating water pipes; it was far too loud for that.

I can't fail to recall the corridor that ran along the ground floor, which I found particularly unnerving. We had to use it because the staff lavatory was located at the end. Other care assistants reported an eerie presence in the corridor. One even claimed to see a man in old-fashioned clothing, wearing a tall hat. I never saw him myself, but I felt his eyes upon my back.

Yes Dear, my years at Cecilia House certainly opened my eyes to the possibility of the paranormal, and not least were we terrified by the attic, and how the hatch would slam shut in the dead of the night. I'm open minded to *anything*.

⁕⁕

After relaying my stories to my daughter, I took a deep breath in as an uneasy feeling slowly crept over me. Even recounting the old tales sent shivers down my spine. The line was quiet.

"Are you there, my love?" I asked. There was no reply from my daughter. I closed my eyes, tiredness catching up with me. *We must have got disconnected*. Suddenly, I felt a warm sensation sweep over my torso, as if someone was tucking a blanket around me, and for some reason my hands and cheeks felt flushed. Then the handset began to ring.

"Hello, Georgina?"

"No, it's Peter. Mum…" his voice wavered. "I've got some terrible news…" My son sobbed down the line. "It's Georgina, I need you to sit down…"

I felt confused. What could warrant his tears?

"I've just been on the phone to her, Peter, she's perfectly –"

"*What?!* That's simply not possible, mum!" he paused, and then continued with a small voice that sounded like it would break at any moment. "Mum," he croaked. "Georgina's been in a fatal accident. Her car overturned on the motorway… she hasn't survived…"

I dropped the handset, and it hung over the dresser, bouncing slightly on its curly wire.

"Georgina! *Ring me back*!" I pleaded, but despite my strongest willing, my beautiful daughter never did return my call. I was grateful, at least, that she had been able to contact me just one final time. I just wish I could have said goodbye, but just like I felt the presence of Cecilia's ghosts all those years ago, I *knew* my Georgina was around, and I told her I loved her every single night before laying my own weary head to rest, until the day would come that I would join her, wherever it was that she had gone.

CLEARWATER BAY

"Hello deary, first time here at Clearwater Bay?" The lady who had been watching me unpack called out from her caravan's sundeck, which was freshly stained in a deep crimson.

"Yes, it's a long-needed getaway for me and my two little ones!" I laughed light-heartedly, but the expression on the woman's face remained stern and unemotional.

"You'll be very comfortable, I'm sure. We know the owner of 'Sea Breeze,'" she remarked, nodding over to our caravan. "He seems like a nice man. He rents this place out over the summer, though there's something a little peculiar about the fellow if I do say so myself…" she pursed her lips, "I've never quite been able to put my finger on it…even after all these years…"

I smiled, though there was also something a little strange about the woman leaning against the spindles of the decking, which I couldn't quite put my own finger on. Her haircut was messy and ruffled. I'd say she was probably about my age, forty, perhaps a touch older, but *definitely* plumper.

"Well, anyway, do your children like dogs?" She abruptly changed the subject. A little King Charles Puppy whizzed out onto the decking before I could confirm whether or not the boys were comfortable, but they both eagerly ran over to the friendly pup who chomped and licked their hands playfully.

"Aww, I want a dog! He's so cute!" chirped my younger son. A few moments later, three young girls approached the caravan. They were scruffy and boyish looking, their clothes hanging off them as if they were ill-fitted hand-me-downs. In fact, the whole caravan was rather dilapidated. There were old toys scattered around, and the front of the van was covered in a fluffy white cobweb-like coating which must have been the seed of some kind of plant blowing in the wind.

"That's our Puppy, Benji. Isn't he just adorable?" said the smallest child as she scooped the little dog up in her arms and pulled Benji close to her, away from my boys.

"Yes, we're very lucky to have little Benji. He's a good boy," said the middle child, who was a little plump too. She turned to my youngest. "Are you a good boy, too?" She looked wide eyed, as if expecting an answer to her unusual question.

"Come on boys, let's go into the caravan and unpack!" I ushered them over towards me. *That family are a little odd to say the least* and I thought to myself that *we'd better try to steer well clear of them!*

"Bye Deary!" the lady called as she hurried back into her own lodgings.

༺༻

The next day

I stood at the sink, the sun blazing through the 'floor to ceiling' window of the caravan, lovingly watching my two children play on the grass outside. Even though we were on holiday, I was still obsessed over having a clean and tidy living space, and dishes could not simply be left. So, adorning my yellow marigolds, I continued the washing up, anxious to finish so we could head to Aberdyfi beach and finally enjoy the sun.

It was the perfect weather for relaxing by the seaside. My two boys were excited; West Wales was a world away from inner city London and the fresh sea air was rejuvenating for us all. I noted the caravan next to ours from where I stood in the kitchen. The little dog wasn't on the decking today, and the children's scooters and balls were no longer scattered over the lawn area. Perhaps they'd left the park already, I wondered. It would have been a shame for them if they had – the weather was glorious and was set to remain so for the rest of the week.

I looked out in the distance towards the Cambrian mountains; the peaks were majestic; it was a beautiful part of the British Isles. I felt lucky we had a chance to visit. We'd seen the advert for the holiday on a social media site. It had been somewhat of a bargain due to a last-minute cancellation. Paying full price for a week in West Wales in summer's peak would have been quite out of the question otherwise.

I smiled to myself. Jack and Dylan were adorable. They played so well together despite the seven-year age gap, and Dylan, being the older brother, really looked after Jack. He was quite the protective big brother. The boys' father was no longer in the picture, and I always felt Dylan took on more than just a brotherly role. He was certainly a great support to me.

"Mam! Mam! Look at me!" Screeched Jack, thrilled that he'd managed three kickie uppies in a row. I called out the window to him.

"*Well done*, Jack! You'll be picked for the school football team in no time, poppet!". I loved to hear the pair of them laughing. I thought to myself how blessed I was to have such well-behaved children. "I'll make you both some squash. You must be thirsty with all that running around!" I stretched to see them out of the tiny window. They didn't reply – too busy having fun and enjoying the sunshine, no doubt. I continued with the dishes, there weren't too many left. I meticulously washed and rinsed the glasses and cutlery, wondering why on earth the caravan itinerary did not include a dish drainer.

It was eerily quiet, despite the windows and the main door behind me being wide open, though I could just make out the squawk of herring gulls from the bay. I took in a deep breath. The sea, the sun, family time – *what complete bliss.*

ملاک

"Mam! Mam!" Cried Jack as he bounded through the open caravan door. Dylan was only moments behind him.

"Where's Mammy?" He said as he hurriedly caught up with his little brother. The boys dived around the caravan in pursuit of their mother.

"Mam! Mam!" Jack raced into the bedroom, but his mother was nowhere to be seen.

ملاک

I held my breath, knowing that if I so much as uttered a single whimper, she'd slit my throat, for I could feel the blade against my skin. Beads of sweat rolled down my forehead as I caught a glimpse of Jack from the small gap between the hinges on the wardrobe door.

"Mam's not here…" He wept. Dylan comforted the small boy. They huddled together on the bed for a moment, in the comfort of each other's arms.

"She's just gone down the shop, don't worry Jack," He ruffled his brother's hair, "It's alright, little dude, don't worry."

I wanted to scream out to them, *"I'm here! I'm here!"* But when she sensed I may try to make myself known, the blade pressed against my neck with more force. I started to shake, and silent tears ran down my cheeks, but no matter my angst, in my desperate situation I clung to the hope of saving my sons. I'm certain had I raised the alarm that something terrible would have happened to them. I could only watch as the two boys scampered out of the caravan, and that was the very last time I ever saw them.

∽∾

The man sat in his house, which overlooked the caravan site. Tall trees almost engulfed the property, and one could easily miss its very presence from down in the valley. His spindly fingers caressed the keyboard as he delicately tapped the letters with a click, click, click.

Beautifully presented caravan available at a bargain price due to last-minute cancellation…

"Deary," his wife called from the kitchen. "Do you fancy a cup of tea?" When he didn't reply, with some difficulty she pulled off the yellow marigolds she had been washing the dishes with. The gloves were a little tight for her. She had to pull them off with quite a tug. *Shame they don't fit*, she murmured under her breath. A little dog started to bark.

"Feed that mutt, will you?" He sniffed, wiping the back of his hand over his sweaty nose.

"He really likes the new fresh meat you've prepared, nothing quite like it, only the good stuff for our Benji," he concurred, and his wife nodded obediently, smiling, as she watched the little pup gobble up his delicious fresh dinner, as if he'd never had a meal quite like it before.

THE STABLE DOOR

Every day and night, Tamsin's eyes (one brown, one blue) would transfix on the old stable door in the scullery. It wasn't actually a stable, so the homeowner, Pearl, had always wondered why the door was split in half, but it provided much amusement for her grandchildren when they came to visit in the summer.

Yet curiously no matter the time of day, Tamsin would often sit, head tilted up, fixated on the door, her tail poised as though she may pounce at any moment, but she never did, she merely watched and waited with a sense of anticipation.

"She's a funny old girl," Pearl said to her neighbour, Barry, (who came around for a cup of tea now and again). He noticed her dog's strange behaviour, though wasn't at all perturbed.

"I've seen dogs do that myself over the years. She might be able to hear the scurrying of tiny mice outside, or, as they get older, dogs can be prone to seeing things that aren't *really* there…" he mused. Pearl tapped his arm playfully.

"Don't be giving me the heebie jeebies, Barry!" she laughed, and then leant down to Tamsin and gave her sweet soft head a stroke.

"Oh, I don't mean to…" he reassured her. "I'm just saying animals can be very sensitive at times…"

Tamsin had come from the local rescue centre, a few months after Pearl's last dog, Megan, had sadly passed away. Pearl would have felt lonely without a four-legged companion, so it was only natural she'd take on another dog, eventually.

Tamsin was a long-haired sheepdog now well into her senior years. When Pearl had arrived at the rescue centre, the pair had been equally drawn to each other and it really had felt as if they were meant to be together. Pearl certainly couldn't imagine life without a dog, especially now her children had grown up and flown the nest.

"She's got the most interesting eyes, bless her. She looks like a wise old girl, but there's a hint of sadness in those eyes too." remarked Barry, slurping his tea down. Pearl nodded.

"She does have beautiful eyes. I knew straight away I would take her home, and she's really settled in, which is reassuring, but she isn't half fascinated with that stable door…"

"Ah, don't worry, it'll be nothing," Barry said, and Tamsin whined.

"*Heterochromia.*" he stated.

"I'm sorry?"

"Heterochromia, it's the medical term for her eyes being different colours."

Pearl had lived in the little country house most of her life, having only moved briefly to London in her twenties. While away in the city, her mother, Freda, tragically passed away, leaving Pearl heartbroken. Pearl's father had been deployed in the armed forces, often being posted away for months on end, and when he heard of his wife's passing, he had become detached, and never returned. Pearl took over the upkeep of the house and had never left since.

To Pearl's dismay, she had little knowledge of her family history; her dear mother had refrained from talking about her grandparents, and Pearl knew only her grandmother's name; Dorothy, yet nothing more.

Upon moving back to the house, Pearl had met her husband in the village and a happy marriage followed, resulting in the birth of their two offspring, and a favourable twenty-five years. Sadly, not long ago, Pearl's husband had passed away unexpectedly. But she was an independent lady, and although missed her husband terribly, she rather enjoyed her now solitary lifestyle – that was, of course, as long as she had a dog in her life, she knew if she did, she would be content.

"Come here, Tammy, my girl," she called Tamsin over. She was an affectionate creature and the two of them had grown close, forming a special bond that seemed so meaningful. There was certainly something remarkable about their friendship. Tamsin slept at the foot of Pearl's bed and barely left her side. It was fair to say that they had become quite inseparable in such a short period of time.

❧☙

One afternoon, Pearl felt a burning desire to clear out some old junk. She had a loft full of 'bric a brac', and goodness knows what else. Much of it had been untouched for an eternity, she'd hasten a guess, for hundreds of years. She'd hate for her children to have to go through the laborious task if she was to suddenly die, and now was as good a time as ever to make a start. Pearl certainly wasn't as agile as she once was, but still managed the ladder and, without too much of a to-do, was able to successfully crawl up through the loft hatch. There, she was faced with what looked like an impossible task, but Pearl was determined to get the job done.

"Now, let's start with this big box…" she murmured to herself, as she dragged one box towards the loft hatch. She cleverly suspended it in a sheet, lowering the parcel to the ground before climbing down the ladder herself. Lugging the box to the table in the kitchen, she wiped away a thick layer of dust. Sitting down in the antique red velvet armchair by the table, (which had seen better days), she opened the box and reached inside. *Old Newspapers, letters, and a bunch of old photographs.* The headlines caught her attention.

'Young women murdered in brutal attack'
and
'Burglary gone awry, resulting in tragic death'

Pearl retrieved one photograph. It was black and white and aged considerably. On the back was the date *1926,* and the name *Dotty Adams*. "Dotty?" Pearl read out loud – *who was that?* She thought, while picking up another photograph of the same very pretty lady with long hair. In this picture, she was holding a baby, and written on the back in black ink was *Baby Freda Adams.* Pearl gasped! *This must be my mother as a 'babe in arms,'* she thought, *and Dotty Adams*, well, of course, it was a picture of her grandmother, Dorothy. She carefully traced her finger across the portrait and hadn't noticed that Tamsin had curled snuggly up beside her legs. Dorothy was beautiful, and although the photograph was not in colour, she couldn't fail to see how stunning her grandmother's features were, especially her eyes.

Pearl continued to read through the paperwork and learnt more about the attack that took place. She discovered it happened *in this very house*. She shook as she realised that her grandmother, Dorothy, had been the victim. Why had her mother never told her about this? It seemed like someone had shut away all the evidence in the attic with the intention to conceal it forever. Pearl began to sob. Tamsin, who was clearly troubled by her distress, began to bark and whine.

"Now, now, Tammy, it's ok, it's alright girl," said Pearl as she patted Tamsin, which calmed the animal down somewhat, but Tamsin still stayed close by Pearl's feet. The old lady browsed through some more papers and found a hand-written letter addressed to Dorothy.

"Oh my," she said out loud, "*A love letter.*" It was written, of course, before Dotty's death, presumably in her husband's hand, (Pearl's grandfather).

"My love, your beauty captivates me, and magic lies within your eyes, one brown, one blue, my darling, I will forever love you."

Pearl glanced to the floor where Tamsin still lay gently against her slippers. *One brown, one blue, how peculiar* Pearl whispered, *that's very odd. My grandma's eyes were just like yours, Tamsin.*

Pearl hurriedly read the next letter in the pile she was clutching. It was written from Dorothy to her husband.

"I sit by the stable door, day after day, eagerly awaiting your return, not knowing how long I will be waiting for, but my dear, beloved, I will wait forever for you, no matter how long it will take, I will be there, waiting for you, my love."

Pearl froze. *Something clicked.* She hadn't realised, but while she had been deep in thought, Tamsin had left her side and ventured into the scullery.

Pearl stood up and steadied herself against the table, for she felt quite taken aback as her mind raced, and she tried to fit together the pieces of the puzzle.

By the time Pearl reached the scullery, she let out an exasperated wail – it was as she had expected. Tamsin sat there, staring at the stable door, eyes transfixed, *waiting*.

"Oh, my!" Pearl couldn't quite help but keep thinking back to the words she had read, about her Grandma having eyes like Tamsin, and not only that, but the fact that a young Dotty had once promised to wait – to wait by the stable door for her husband to return – *forever*.

There was a knock on the front door, which gave Pearl a fright. She peeped through the spyhole and saw that it was Barry. She unlocked the chain and pulled open the door.

"Oh, Barry, I'm so glad to see you! You won't believe it, but I've found some old letters and newspaper cuttings, and I might be getting a bit carried away but I–I…" she trailed off, interrupted by the sound of Tamsin barking like mad at the stable door.

"Oh, my!" Pearl gasped, "What on earth could the matter be?"

They rushed back into the kitchen, through to the scullery, where they came to Tamsin who was jumping up at the stable door, her tail wagging with an energy Pearl had never seen Tamsin express before.

"Is there someone on the other side of the door?" Barry bounded towards Tamsin and lifted the latch of the stable door, expecting to see the postman or milkman, but there was no one there. Pearl smiled. She passed the letters that she had found to Barry, and noted that Tamsin was now relaxed and peaceful, lying down with her eyes gently closed. She knelt and softly stroked Tamsin from her head across her back.

"I think he came home, Barry. Dotty no longer must wait…"

"Who?" a perplexed Barry asked.

"Never mind, Barry, but I think Tamsin will be a lot less interested in that stable door from here on out…"

BUTTERED TOAST

I lay on the reclining chair, feeling numb; a hot wheat bag strategically positioned on my tummy. The nurse brought me buttery toast and my stomach moaned. I couldn't believe I'd done it, but God, did I *need* that toast. I bit into the first slice, sucking up the juicy butter; oh *I ached*, craving the calories. Despite my undoubted relief, all I could think of was how disappointed my mother would be if she ever found out what I'd done.

"Here you are, love," the nurse handed me a little paper cup with two pills. I smiled.

"Thanks," I said, followed by a sigh. "When can I go home?"

༺༻

Katie's screams were intolerable. They cut right through me.

"*Shut up, just shut up,*" I said out loud, with aggression in my voice. I couldn't stand the noise. It grated on me something terrible; made my blood boil. Eighteen months of this incessant screaming would surely be enough to tip anyone off the edge? I kept asking myself why would anyone ever even consider having a second child? I paced up and down the landing, the tension rising in my head. It was 2am, and I was desperate for sleep, but my relationship with slumber was distant, and to tell you the truth, I didn't like what living without it had turned me into. I heard Ewen mumble from the bedroom.

"Seren, what you doing?" his melodic Welsh accent was prominent. I loved it so much.

"It's Katie," I whispered back. "Don't worry, I'll deal with it. Go back to sleep."

I slumped back down by the door frame to Katie's room and felt dizzy as I watched the colourful stars circle around the ceiling. The projector was a gift from my mother-in-law to mark Katie's birth. I shuddered when I thought of the woman. She always put me down and never ceased to be critical of my parenting.

I felt terrible, utterly exhausted. I'd only been home from the hospital a few days, barely having a chance to build up my strength. I closed my eyes and tried not to think of the trauma of it all. At least Katie seemed to have settled now, so I snuck back into my bedroom and climbed into my soft, warm bed. Curling up on my side and facing the wall, I hadn't realised that Ewan was still awake. He shuffled closer and cuddled into me before his hand made its way to my tummy. He stroked my empty belly affectionately and kissed me on the neck.

"Oh Seren, I can't believe in just six months, we'll have another one! You're the best mother ever. *I just can't wait…*"

HOW CAN I HELP YOU?

Arthur watched the small digital clock on the side of his PC monitor. Each minute dragged as he longed for his shift in the call centre to draw to an end. *Just a few hours to go*, he thought. What was once a busy bustling environment was now a cold, lonely and isolated space. Arthur wished he could work from home like the rest of his colleagues, but he lived so far out in the sticks where the internet connection was so unreliable that it would be impossible to connect to the work network for any period of time.

He shivered. He was getting too old for this. Despite the pandemic, commuting from the sleepy village of Somersby every day into the city of Broadwell was really becoming too much for the nearly sixty-year-old Arthur. He counted down the days to retirement, as well as the hours to the end of his shift. What made it even worse was that nobody was calling – it was deadly quiet. The pandemic had hit everyone hard, and people just weren't ordering expensive designer kitchens in the current climate. He handled a couple of calls an hour, if that. He flicked through the pages of his magazine, *History Today*. Arthur was a bit of a history buff, even if he did say so himself.

Arthur smiled as he recollected the call he had received from a dear old lady earlier on that day, which had cheered him up. Though Gwen wasn't interested in upgrading her kitchen, in fact, she hadn't even seemed to realise she was calling a kitchen and bathroom firm at all, and they ended up having a good old natter about this and that; they even had a shared interest in history. Arthur really rather liked her. It seemed they also had something else in common – she sounded dreadfully lonely too.

The call centre was situated in the old part of the city, and although the offices had been modernised somewhat, the building was still old-fashioned and felt cold at the best of times. Every day Arthur brought in a blanket with him which he draped over his shoulders. He found without the heat of the other bodies in the room that he felt a chill, and it seemed to be getting worse as each day went on. Finally, his shift was over. His office was on the ground floor, so he didn't have far to go before he was out on the street and making his way to his car.

Arthur lived alone. He heated up his beef stroganoff and watched an episode of 'Tony Robinson's Time Team' before crunching on some peanut M&Ms. He yawned. It was nine o'clock and time for him to retire to the bedroom. Each evening was much of a muchness, and the pandemic meant Arthur was lonelier than ever. His only companion had passed away earlier last year. Arthur had been devastated to bury Randolf the cat in his garden at the beginning of lockdown. It was the lowest of times that Arthur had ever faced.

The next day arrived, and Arthur was up early, making his cheese and pickle sandwiches before setting off to work. Arthur, being a keen historian, had already carried out a lot of research about the market town he lived in. To ease his boredom at work, he thought he might do some research on the old city of Broadwell in between calls. He sat himself down, adjusted his headset and logged into the systems, before pressing the button to make himself ready to take a call. To his surprise, the phone beeped in his ear immediately.

"Good morning. Thank you for calling Merlin's kitchens and bathrooms. You're through to Arthur. How can I help?" Arthur was most taken aback, as it was unusual for a call to come through so early.

"Oh Arthur, I'm so glad that you answered. It's Gwen! We were talking yesterday." The lady beamed. Remembering the pleasant, but rather chatty lady he had previously spoken to, he relaxed.

"Ah yes, I do indeed Gwen, how can I help you?"

"Oh, you *are* observant to remember me, Arthur, but I'm calling to make a complaint – I had an *extremely* bad night last night."

Arthur hesitated. *A bad night?* He didn't have a response to that query in his script. He pulled his blanket over him, noting that the chill seemed to be more prevalent in the morning.

"Oh, dear, I am sorry to hear that, Gwen."

"Well, what are you going to do about it? I didn't sleep well. There's too much noise."

"That's not good, Gwen. We all need a good night's sleep. I wish there was something I could do to help…"

"They're banging *all night long*, Arthur. I need you to make it *stop!*" The urgency in her voice was quite unnerving, and Arthur was really confused. *What did she mean, make it stop?* He began to think it must be a hoax, or that the lady was not of sound mind. He distanced the earpiece away from his head for a moment. Gwen's voice was coming down the receiver a little too loudly and a little too clearly…

"Arthur, are you still there?!"

"Ahem, yes, Gwen. Have you got a family member that can help Gwen? I'm not sure what exactly I can do."

"No dear," she droned, "They're all dead and gone, been six feet under for donkeys. I'm on my own, you see, just like you, Arthur, but they just won't stop banging and I can't get any rest, dear."

The line broke up. *How did she know I'm alone?* Arthur asked himself. He must have mentioned it in their previous conversation. He racked his mind to remember, but his memory was not like it used to be.

"Gwen, are you there?" Arthur asked, but the line was distorted with some kind of static interference. Arthur ended the call and shook his head. *I hope the old dear's alright,* he thought.

Arthur willed the day away, and strangely, it did seem to go unusually faster than normal. He left at four thirty on the dot, leaving his blanket on the chair behind him by mistake, and made his way out of the office. Once home, he warmed up his chicken supreme and watched an episode of 'Lucy Worsley's Royal Palace Secrets' and finished the remaining M&Ms. He hadn't seemed to have time to do any research on Broadwell that day – the day had flown by, not that he was complaining. *I'll try again tomorrow,* he supposed.

Arthur woke up bright and early, prepared his corned beef salad, and made his way into the call centre. He set up his computer and checked his empty mailbox, and yet again, he immediately received a call.

"Good morning. Thank you for calling Merlin's kitchens and bathrooms. You're through to Arthur. How can I help?"

"Arthur! You *are* here!" It was his team leader, Sara. "I was trying to get through to you *all* day yesterday, but you didn't answer or respond to any of my emails?!"

Arthur looked at his inbox again, and this time he saw that he had indeed received numerous emails from his concerned manager throughout yesterday's shift. *That's strange. I could have sworn ....*

"I also called you and left multiple messages on your mobile phone."

Arthur examined his phone and, sure enough, he saw six missed calls and the little envelope icon was displayed to indicate he had an outstanding message. *How strange,* he thought. *I didn't hear any calls come through…*

"*And,* what's more, Arthur, I came down to the office myself to find you weren't even there! *What on earth* is going on, Arthur!?"

Flabbergasted, Arthur paused to gather his thoughts. He *had* been in the office all day; he *hadn't* left early, as Sara had suggested. He left at four thirty, not a minute earlier. Arthur reached for his blanket behind his chair, suddenly feeling the draft, then realised it was not there.

"My blanket –"

"*Arthur*! Where were you, and why were you not responding to my calls or emails?" demanded his boss.

Arthur, in a daze, failed to reply. He spun around on his office chair and caught sight of his blanket strewn over one of the soft seats and to add to his confusion it looked like somebody, or *something* was underneath it, in fact whatever the blanket was covering looked like the distinct shape of a person.

"ARTHUR!" came the manager's voice before Arthur ripped the headset off and scuttled over to where his blanket lay, and with one sweeping movement, he grabbed it away to reveal – *nothing*. He scratched his head. His mind was definitely playing tricks on him. He rushed back to his desk, almost falling over his own two feet, and fumbled with the headset.

"Hello? Sara? I'm sorry, I can't explain…"

"It's not Sara, darling, it's Gwen. Have you forgotten me already? Now listen – *why* didn't you stop the banging, dear?"

"What?" Arthur murmured.

"I did something for you, Arthur. I know how lonely you are here on your own, and how you can't wait to get home, and just what do I get in return, huh? Diddly squat, that's what!" Gwen pressed on.

Arthur turned white and started to breathe rapidly, and at the same time, his mobile phone started to ring. Sara's name came up on the digital display.

"I've got to go –" he said to Gwen.

"Before you do, Arthur – it was very kind of you to leave me a blanket, but *you've got to stop the noise.*"

With that, Arthur disconnected the call and answered his mobile phone.

"Sara, I'm not feeling well. I need to take the day off…" Arthur felt unusually dizzy and disoriented. He thought to himself that he must be coming down with a fever, perhaps he had finally succumbed to the virus. He had read somewhere that hallucinations could be a symptom. He concluded he would go home and call the GP. Perhaps he was just having a bit of a senior moment, but even so, he wanted to be sure.

That night, Arthur left a message with the Doctor, and then proceeded to heat up his sausage and bean casserole, but he didn't watch any TV. Instead, he wanted to take his mind off the strange goings on at work, so he booted up his ancient desktop computer and spent some time doing what he loved the most, researching history. Broadwell was not a part of the country he was overly familiar with. Although he worked there, he knew little about its past. He began with the area where he worked and discovered that the city was rich with history, and he relished in making notes as he learned about the part the city played in smuggling and overseas trade.

Interesting, he thought. He pinned down the building where the call centre was located. He had known the building was old, but he hadn't quite realised it was *that* old. Over one hundred years, that was impressive. He studied aerial photographs and researched the location with great interest.

Suddenly, he stopped. *What?* The building was once the site of a psychiatric hospital!? Well now; he had never known that! It was certainly of interest. He continued to read, starting to feel uneasy as he learned about the kind of things that went on when the hospital was operational. It seemed it had been quite a frightening place, and the patients there had been subjected to what could now only be considered as inhumane conditions. *This is where I work?* Arthur said out loud, very much troubled by the thought. Further to this, he came across first hand witness statements about the terrible noises that were frequently heard from within the institution. It was horrifying to think that people were just left, sectioned off in small rooms with nothing to do but shout and frantically bang on the walls.

His mobile phone rang, distracting him from his research.

"Art! It's Robin, from work."

"Oh, hello Robin, how are you?"

"I'm good mate, just at work. Listen, I just had a call from Gwen…" explained Robin. "She came through to the customer service line, hoping to reach you."

"Oh, yes?" Arthur took in a deep breath, feeling sick with anxiety.

"She says she wants to know when you're coming back. She's feeling lonely and frightened. The old dear sounded ever so worried, mate. She wouldn't leave a number, but she wants you to come back – she says she's going mad, all alone, and the noise hasn't stopped. Does this make *any* sense at all to you, Art?"

After a brief reflection, Arthur replied.

"Yes, Robin, yes it does…"

Arthur was stunned, his stomach churned; he didn't feel well enough to go back to work that week. In fact, he never did go back to the office, as if by a miracle his internet service provider updated the broadband cables in his area and he was soon upgraded to super-fast cable broadband, which enabled him to start working from home.

By the time the pandemic was finally over, a few years later, Arthur was able to hang up his call centre boots for good. He now spent most of his days watching history documentaries and even got himself a new furry companion, a rescue spaniel called Herbert. Life was comfortable and before long Arthur met a lovely lady on an online dating app for the over sixties. In a short time, his lady friend Florence moved in, and they were all set for a peaceful retirement.

Arthur went out every morning with Herbert to collect his daily newspaper from the local newsagents. He whistled happily as he waddled along, looking forward to his eggs on toast that Florence, like clockwork, would always cook for him. He noted Broadwell was in the news; the headline stated that there'd been a spate of break-ins including some of the old offices; he was glad he wasn't going into the city anymore. Herbert bounded through the door, and sure as night follows day there was Florence bent over the stove, making him the most perfect and delicious scrambled eggs, and he could even smell bacon wafting through the kitchen too.

He glanced at the table, and noted there were three places laid, instead of the usual two.

"Are we expecting company?" he chuckled, placing the newspaper down on the table and pulling out a chair.

"Oh, Arthur – *we are*!" she beamed. "It's your old friend, Gwen! She said she's been trying to track you down for ages," she paused, "And she mentioned something about unfinished business –she's just using the bathroom, she'll be down in a moment!"

Arthur turned white and gripped the arms of the chair. Florence gestured towards the kettle.

"Well, don't just sit there, you silly old thing, it's just boiled. Make your old friend a nice cup of tea!"

SOPHIE'S SHELL

The weather was glorious, with not one cloud in the sky, and temperatures were set to soar into the mid-twenties. Sophie and her family were having a 'beach day'. Sophie watched as her mother smeared sunblock all over her baby brother before adorning him in a wide-brimmed sun hat and setting him loose with a bucket and a spade.

She glanced over at dad; he had assembled the sun tent, securing it with pegs, and he had neatly laid down the beach towels. He seemed rather pleased with himself as he placed the picnic basket in the corner of the tent and tied a little Union Jack flag to the top of the structure.

Looks like we're settling in for the day, thought Sophie. This would undoubtedly be the worst day of the holidays. Sophie hated the beach. Suddenly Sophie's thoughts were disturbed by a spadeful of flying sand which landed all over her. She squinted her eyes and glared at the culprit.

"*Archie*, you little brat!" She yelled, shaking the sand out of her hair. "That's it! I'm not sitting around here all day. I'm going for a walk!"

Sophie's parents, (Charlena and Mitchell), sighed with relief. They were ultimate sun worshippers and were looking forward to some peace and quiet. Dad would watch baby Archie while mum lay in the sun, and vice versa, and it would be a lot more relaxing without teenage Sophie moaning for the entire day.

"Have a lovely walk, sweetie," her mother called as Sophie walked away in a strop, she then turned to her husband. "Right, Mitchell, rub that lotion on my back, won't you!"

"Yes, right away!"

Sophie stomped off as quickly as she could, but the sand was too soft and too hot on her bare feet, making it impossible to walk with any speed or elegance.

"Ugh, I just *hate* my little brother! I wish he'd never been born!" she scorned to herself. Ever since Archie had been born, he had been the centre of attention and her parents, who, although were not particularly selfless with either of their children, now paid even less attention to Sophie.

The soft sand continued to make walking quite burdensome, so Sophie made a sharp right turn and headed towards the sea. She carefully nipped in and out of the many colourful tents that were strewn across the beach until finally, she arrived at the comfortable and easier to negotiate flat wet sand.

"That's better. I really hate the beach. Nothing interesting ever happens," she said to herself. She'd much rather be back at the caravan watching TV or, even better, playing on her PlayStation.

"*I hate holidays.*" she cussed, "next year I think I'll just stay at home!"

Sophie winced as the shallow ripples of sea water met her toes; the water was freezing cold despite the warmth of the air. Her parents came to Cornwall *every year*. It was so boring. Her friend, Keelie, had flown off to Greece, Sammy to Florida, and she was stuck in *Cornwall*, where absolutely nothing exciting was ever bound to happen.

As her feet became accustomed to the chill of the wild Atlantic Ocean, she sat down in a position where the waves met only her lower legs. She dug her toes into the sand and gazed out into the ocean. It was only eleven thirty in the morning, but the beach was filling up, and the sea was bubbling over with body boarders and screaming children. She watched a little girl have a full-blown tantrum with her dad over a sandcastle that had been washed away by the sea.

'*Don't build it so near to the waves then, brat,*' thought Sophie. She observed a gaggle of forty-five or so year old women in bikinis, *who really shouldn't be in bikinis,* she said under her breath. Then, she took note of a girl, probably about her own age, swimming in and out of the waves, seemingly having a wonderful time. In fact, she looked quite confident, and beautiful, too. Many of the boys were admiring her. Sophie sighed as she laid her eyes among a multitude of other families splashing around having fun – *urgh,* thought Sophie, *I hate the beach.*

☙❧

"Ah, that's nice, we can really relax now that Sophie is out of our hair!" said mum, who was lying on her back with enormous sunglasses covering her eyes.

"Yes, dear, this is *the life.*" Mitchell peered over his newspaper to check on baby Archie, who was still enjoying tossing sand here, there, and everywhere.

"Why don't you take him for a paddle, love, while I get some shuteye."

"Yes, dear," he yawned, "I'll just finish this article. Apparently, there's been lots of strange items from the tropics washed up in Cornwall, and also an infestation of poisonous jellyfish in Tenerife."

Mum sighed, "Thank goodness we don't get any of those in Cornwall. You can't beat a staycation!"

~~~

Sophie lay down on her back, now gazing upwards into the sky. She flailed out her arms combing the sand around her.

"Ouch!" she shrieked when her fingers came across something hard and spiky. She jumped! Sitting up in shock, she turned to her side to see what it was she had accidentally touched. There was something sharp buried in the sand. She carefully dug it out.

Sophie studied the object; she had never seen a shell like it on the beach in Cornwall in all the years she had been dragged down there. It was so large a shell that she couldn't conceal it in her palm, and it had several large spikes protruding from it, with a thick smooth lip. It glistened and gleamed, even without the sunshine, and its surface sported colourful swirls that seemed to move whenever it was turned. It was *so* beautiful, but didn't look like it belonged on a beach in Cornwall. Sophie held it up in front of her and flicked the sand off it. *What a prize,* she thought, as she watched it sparkle in the sunlight.

"*You found my shell!*"

Out of nowhere a young girl appeared next to Sophie, who had been so engrossed in her find she hadn't even noticed her approaching.

"*Your* shell? I don't think so," smirked Sophie, who wasn't prepared to give up her treasure so easily.

"Yes, I've been looking for it all morning. It's very special to me," the girl said. Sophie studied her.

"You're the girl I've been watching swimming. You've not been looking for *anything*! You've been out there in the sea without a care!"

Sophie's Shell among other curious tales

"Just because I've been swimming doesn't mean that's not my shell and I've not been looking for it!" The girl looked sorrowful. Her green eyes gazed out at the ocean. She swept her long blond hair away from her face.

"So you won't give it back?" the girl asked.

Sophie shook her head firmly. "No."

"I need to go. Be careful with my shell, won't you?" The girl ran off with speed. Sophie tried to follow which direction she had gone but lost track of her among the many other people on the beach, but she thought she may have seen her re-enter the water.

What's so special about this stupid shell, anyway?

Sophie's tummy rumbled. It was true; she hadn't wanted to be reunited with her baby brother so soon, but the thought of her tuna and sweetcorn sandwiches, salt and vinegar crisps and snack bar was just too tempting. So, with her hunger getting the better of her, she padded back to her family. As she approached their tent, things didn't look right. Instead of her mum sprawled out catching the sun rays, both mum and dad were standing up with their hands in the air as if they were arguing. This was strange, she thought. Mum and dad may be self-centred, but they *never* argued. It was then she realised that Archie was missing from the scene and once she was within hearing distance; she caught exactly what her mother was saying.

"You flaming *idiot*! You should have been watching him, not falling asleep, you bloody halfwit!" cried mum. Sophie's dad looked from left to right, sweat pouring down his face. He tried to speak, but mum was relentless.

"You've blinking lost our son! You better get out there and find him, Mitchell. I'll be right here. *Just find our son!*"

Sophie ran over to her parents.

"Mum, Dad, you've lost Archie?!"

Mum was already laid back down on her front.

"Dad?" Sophie spat, with her hands on her hips.

"Sophie, love, I've got to find Archie. You'll help me, won't you?"

"I *hate* that little brat. He's always stealing the limelight! But Dad – *you fell asleep?*!"

"Sophie, he's your brother. We need to find him. He's just a baby, and this beach is full of danger. How would you feel if you never saw your baby brother again?"

Sophie considered this for a while. She didn't like Archie one bit. All he did was dribble, and make a mess, oh and cry, *all the time*. Yet, for a moment, she imagined never seeing him again, and drew in a deep breath.

"I would feel dreadful! *We need to find him*!"

"I'll go down to the shoreline," said Dad. "You search the top of the beach, and *alert* the lifeguard, and Sophie, what's that you've got in your hand?"

"*This?*" she said, holding up the shell. "Oh, this, it's just something I found buried in the sand…"

❧ ☙

By now, the news had spread over the beach that a little boy was missing, and several members of the public accompanied dad, while Sophie went off to search the top side of the beach as dad had requested, still clutching her shell.

"*Brat!!! Where are you?*" she called, scanning the beach as she pushed through the sand, her heels sinking in as she ploughed forward. There were plenty of screaming brats everywhere, but as soon as she got close enough to check their faces, she soon realised that none of them were her baby brother. She stopped momentarily and wiped her brow. It was getting unbearably hot, and there was absolutely no sign of Archie. For the first time, she started to feel slightly concerned.

As she moved on, she heard a strange murmur from within the dunes which lined the top of the beach. Surreptitiously, she slipped away from the beach and climbed up into the dunes through the long grass, lulled towards the sound of a girl singing.

"*It's you!*" Sophie exclaimed as she spotted the same girl she'd spoken to on the beach earlier. She was sitting with her legs buried in the sand, waving a blade of sea grass around nonchalantly. The girl looked up, surprised.

"*Oh*, my shell!"

"Is that *all* you can think about? Haven't you heard? My baby brother's lost. Even though I hate him, he could be in all sorts of trouble. He could have been kidnapped!"

"I'll tell you what. If you give me my shell back, I'll help you find him?"

Sophie had to think carefully about this. She held the shell up, and tried to weigh up what she wanted more – *baby Archie, Mysterious Shiny Shell, baby Archie, Mysterious Shiny Shell*, she mused, before tossing the shell to the girl.

"Oh have it, I've got no use for your silly shell anyway, and now you've got to help me find my little brother!"

The pair ran off into the crowds, scouring the beach for baby Archie, calling his name, and asking everyone they saw if they had seen a baby boy. After a short time, Sophie spun around to realise that the girl was no longer there.

"*Oh great*, I knew I should have kept that shell!" Sophie spat with anger. "That's the last time I trust a random stranger!"

❦

Reunited with dad, a crowd of spectators swarmed at the edge of the water, a man with binoculars bellowed out to the crowds.

"I can see him! He's on a blow up lilo, right out to sea!"

Sure enough, Sophie could just about make out a pink inflatable with a small child clinging on to the sides and she could faintly make out the sound of her brother whimpering.

"*Archie!*" she cried.

"What can we do?! It's too far to swim," she heard a bystander remark.

"Help is on its way," Sophie's dad reassured the woman. "My daughter's alerted the lifeguard."

Sophie's heart sank. She had forgotten to raise the alarm – but *surely* someone else on the beach had done so by now?

"*Daddy*!" squealed Sophie. "Archie's going to die out there!"

They hugged, and at that moment, mum came running down from her sunbathing spot.

"*What's going on*?" She asked, and as she received the details that her baby son was afloat in the middle of the ocean on a pink lilo, she turned white.

"I– I think I need to lie down," and in that moment, Sophie's mum fell to the ground. Dad immediately fell to his knees at her side.

"Charlena, darling, wake up," dad slapped her around the face a few times, and she began to stir.

"Is it all a bad dream?" she mumbled.

Sophie ran into the sea, and waded through the small waves, then she dangerously dived in and fought against the strong incoming tide.

"Sophie, *no*!" cried Dad as he instinctively dived in after her. Mum still lay on the beach in a comatose state.

Concerned onlookers talked among themselves.

"I say, they're going to get into trouble if they're not careful…" they muttered.

What happened next was all rather a blur. The local news reporter had arrived and was snapping away with her camera. Others had attempted to follow the pair into the sea. Some had even got in their own inflatables and attempted to paddle out to rescue baby Archie, but baby Archie and the pink inflatable could no longer be seen.

It was a tragedy. Every witness was sobbing. Dad and Sophie, exhausted, had managed to swim back to the beach, but without Archie, their efforts were thwarted, their hearts empty, their feelings numb.

"What's that noise?" Sophie gasped. She heard a familiar cry of a baby. She'd know that cry anywhere. There was no mistaking that whingey, unbearable moan of her baby brother. She swung around, her eyes darted about, and finally she pinpointed the ghastly sound.

"*Archie*!" she screamed. Her mum, now coming around from the shock, bounded up the beach a few hundred metres to where baby Archie sat innocently playing with the sand, quite unaware he was the cause of all the fuss.

"Oh, *Archie*, my dear darling boy!" mum wailed as she went to scoop him up, but before she did, she noticed something peculiar in his hand.

"What's that he's got, Mitchell?"

It was the mysterious shiny shell! Sophie's jaw dropped. She lunged for him.

"That's mine, *brat!*"

༺ ༻

The story was all over the local news, it even made the nationals, but what was most curious was the News Reporter's video footage, and what had been captured in it. It really was a mystery, and quite unexplainable, yet unmistakably *clear*. Out in the ocean, not far from baby Archie floating on the pink inflatable, a beautiful green fluke lobtailed elegantly out of the water.

Sophie changed her mind about Cornwall; she changed her mind about her brother too, and every time she doubted those feelings (even just a tiny bit), she'd raise her beautiful shell (which she'd since learnt was a Conch shell) to her ear, to remind herself of her mysterious seaside-friend.

For the shell, like many shells, was packed to the brim with magic, and this unusual specimen, having once belonged to a mermaid, was of particular interest. Sophie had come to realise that through it, she had the power to hear the singing of her unexpected acquaintance, just as she did on that hot summer's day, when Sophie found her hiding in the dunes with her legs (or tail) buried in the sand.

DIG DEEPER

Livvy shot up from her bed in the dead of the night, dripping with sweat, her boyfriend, Chris, by her side. It was two am, and these nightmares had been plaguing her at this time like clockwork for the last ten days or so. Chris attempted to comfort his girlfriend, but she was in such a state of unrest, gasping for breath and clutching her chest. It was awful to witness; he reached for his mobile phone, concerned that he might need to call 999 this time, but Livvy's breath began to steady, and she seemed to be slowly coming around.

Chris took a deep sigh of relief. He turned the bedside light on and noted that the little pile of Victorian coins that Livvy had recently found whilst metal detecting had once again been knocked off the table. He wished she'd put them somewhere for safekeeping.

"Chris, I–I've had it again, that same …" she shuddered. "That same *horrible, horrible* dream…" she whimpered, clearly very much affected by the night terror. Chris stroked her earthy coloured hair affectionally in an attempt to soothe her.

"I'm worried about you. You must see the doctor again. Hopefully, the blood tests will come back soon."

"Yeah, but *why* do I keep having this dream, Chris?"

"I don't know..."

"They are always so *real*. It's dark, there's rain, I hear the bray of a horse, and then – suddenly, I can't *breathe*, I'm spinning around and around and –"

"And then you wake, like this, unable to breathe. I can see how terrified you are. There must be something bothering you – what's going on, Liv?"

"I really don't know, but I'm getting a really strong feeling that I need to go back to that farm..."

༺༻

Ten days earlier, Livvy was up at the break of dawn. She'd got all her metal detecting equipment ready, including her find pouch, pin pointer, spade, gloves, and, of course, her beloved detector itself. All detectorists wore camo. She had never worked out exactly why, but it was a thing. Livvy packed everything in the car and was really looking forward to a day out on the field with the Somerset History Finders' Metal Detecting association. The weather forecast predicted a dry day with little chance of a shower, although the ground was saturated with previous rainfall, which was the best condition for treasure hunting.

After the usual briefing, (where the organiser explained what fields they had access to, and predictably reminded everyone to fill their holes properly), they were off. The swarm of detectorists soon disbanded over the one-hundred-and-fifty-acre permission. Soon they were appropriately scattered over the fields. Although detectorists were social when they wanted to be, once out detecting, as a general rule, they were solitary creatures. She'd catch up with her close friend Mickey after lunch. Her first signal produced a beautiful high-pitched tone, but it was accompanied by the dreaded 'iron grunt'. *I'm not digging that*, she thought to herself. She continued to swing until her coil glided over another target, and this one sounded *so* sweet. She passed the coil over it quickly. It was repeatable and steady, showing a solid number thirty on the display. This was *definitely* a target she must recover. Livvy pushed the spade in to the ground, making a three-sided shape that she could just flick open like a little trap door. Kneeling, she then inserted the handheld pin pointer into the hole, and it beeped straight away. *Nice!* Using the small trowel which was attached to Livvy's belt, she carefully excavated the earth.

There was an edge! It looked round, too. Livvy, with her gloves on, carefully retrieved the item. She sighed. It was just a squashed bottle top, like the type one might have found on the top of an old-fashioned milk bottle. She popped it in her scrap bag and went on her merry way. The morning continued in quite the same manner, scrap after scrap, the occasional small pewter button, and a lucky (?) horseshoe.

True to the forecast, the weather had held up. Livvy was just about to give up and find a tree stump to stop and eat her chicken tikka sandwich, when she came across an irresistible signal. Again, repeatable, and solid, there was no doubt about it – *she was digging it!* Once again, down on her knees, and plastered in thick sticky mud, she put the pin pointer in the hole and moved it around, but just couldn't pick up the signal. She reached for the detector and swung it over the hole and, as clear as crystal, the original signal was produced. *This is a deep one*, mused Livvy as she continued to dig deeper. After a short time, Livvy's pin pointer started to bleep…

A wave of nausea swept over her for a second, and then as she overturned the next spadeful of earth, what she saw literally took her breath away! There in the clod was not one, not two, but at least five or six coins! Not any old coins either. She was sure that they were silver. Excitedly, she retrieved them and on closer inspection; she confirmed they were

Victorian. In fact, the spill comprised of two half crowns, a couple of twopence, a threepence, among a few copper pennies that had certainly seen better days. But the milled silvers were painstakingly beautiful! Although not a particularly old discovery, Livvy was delighted – the Victorian era was a period that she was very much interested in, and her mother, Rosie, had beautifully documented information and photographs from her side of the family in scrapbooks that were a joy to look through.

Livvy was categorically buzzing with her find, it was a real treasure to her. Her heart started beating quickly as she imagined who had dropped the coins and, under what circumstances, they had been lost. Out of nowhere, she felt an enormous thrust upon her as though she had been punched in the stomach, and then proceeded to struggle for breath. She'd had childhood asthma before, so put it down to that, coupled with the adrenaline rush from the find, but when it didn't pass quickly, she felt somewhat concerned. The shortness of breath was quite frightening, and the waves of nausea didn't ease off either. Livvy looked around the field, and to her dismay, couldn't see any of her fellow detectorists anywhere. *Typical,* she thought. At that moment, the skies turned dark, and an unusual sepia ambience filled the air and space around her.

Livvy reached for her mobile phone from one of the many pockets in her various pouches strapped around her waist, leg, and back. She attempted to ring Mickey, but the signal was non-existent. (Mobile network was sketchy at the best of times in these remote locations). *Where were all the other detectorists?* She asked herself once more, but when the heavens suddenly opened, she quickly dropped the Victorian coins into her finds box and made a dash for the hard standing in the farmyard, realising that thankfully the feeling of anxiety and shortness of breath had passed.

With pure elation, Livvy reached her car, opened the driver's side, and collapsed in the seat, leaving the door ajar. She leaned her head back, closed her eyes, and took a deep breath. *Where did that weather come from?* She pondered. The nose of Livvy's car was facing the entrance to the field, and she was startled when Mickey (who was completely dry) playfully knocked on the bonnet.

"Mickey!" she let out a yelp. "You scared me! Where have you been? I couldn't see you anywhere. I couldn't see *anyone!*"

"I could ask you the same thing!" he said. Looking at how soaking wet she was, he enquired. *"Where have you been?* Did you fall in the river or something?"

Livvy looked up into the sky. It was bright and clear, and there were no puddles on the ground. She looked into the field where she saw dozens of detectorists still out on the pasture. Shaking her head, she grabbed onto Mickey's hand a little too tightly and gasped.

"What's going on?"

※※

Livvy and Chris sat at the kitchen table. They had just received a call from the doctors following Livvy's blood tests.

"You've got to listen to the professionals, Liv. Your blood tests are all normal. This has all got to be down to stress… you need to take things easy from now on… and that means *no more detecting…*"

"But –"

"But nothing. You need to go back to bed. And I, sadly, must go to work, but promise me, you'll rest today?"

"Yes, ok," Livvy obediently nodded, but she had no intention of doing so. What Livvy hadn't explicitly explained to Chris was that she had been getting the overwhelming urge to go back to the spot where she found the Victorian coins ten days ago, and it had been getting so strong that she could no longer pretend it wasn't there. Chris kissed her on the head and closed the front door behind him. Livvy rang Mickey right away.

"Mickey, I need your help. I need to get back on that field. Do you have the contact details for the farmer?"

"Yes, I know William and Mary pretty well, and it was my club dig. Let's go together. I'll pick you up in an hour."

The pair pulled up to the farmyard, and the smell of the countryside wafted up their noses. It was another dry day, but time wasn't on their side, and they were hoping the landowners would let them back on site. Before they got out of Mickey's jeep, he looked at Livvy and asked.

"What are you expecting to get out of this?"

"I don't know, Mickey, but some things telling me there's more in that hole to be found…"

They walked gingerly over to the farmhouse and tapped on the door. After a few moments, a grey-haired lady wearing a pinny, covered in flour, opened the solid oak door.

"Oh, hello, Mickey, oh you've popped in at a rather perfect time, it's '*baking day*' Come on in!" she beamed. Livvy and Mickey found themselves being treated to tea, complemented with freshly baked scones and jam, and it really was rather delicious, especially as neither had eaten any breakfast that morning.

"So, Mary – Livvy and I were at the metal detecting event a few weeks ago, and Livvy found a number of Victorian coins, but we think there might be more there… are you happy for us to go and have a further look today?"

Mary stuffed half a scone into her mouth. Nodding, she gestured with her hand towards the fields.

"Yes, yes, for you, anytime, but be careful out there. She's been quite active out there recently…"

"*What?*" chimed Mickey and Livvy in unison.

"Oh, our resident ghost, my dear. Charlotte." She said, without battering an eyelid as if it were quite normal. "Hmmmm, these are rather a nice batch, aren't they…" Mary smacked her lips together in approval.

"Mary, a *ghost*?" gulped Livvy.

"Oh yes, dear, rumour has it the poor soul came to a rather grizzly end, out on the south field," she nodded again, and Livvy and Mickey weren't sure if it was because of her statement or further appreciation for the scones. "Yes, there used to be a bridle way down there…"

"She's right, I looked up the field on an old maps website, Livvy," concurred Mickey.

"So, you don't seem too perturbed about this…erm '*ghost*', Mary?" pried Livvy, with a panic-stricken look on her face.

"Well, dear, when she wants to be heard, she really wants to be heard, just be careful out there, I didn't want you to have any nasty surprises… although, by the looks of it – am I right in saying you've already had an encounter?"

"Well, not exactly…." murmured Livvy.

"Rumour has it, someone murdered the poor soul out there, back in the early 1900s. Young women who have been on the farm have sometimes 'felt' it…"

"*Felt it?*" asked Livvy with trepidation, reflecting on the strange things she had felt since her first visit to the South field.

"Yes, like the air's being sucked out of them, like they're being starved of oxygen… rumour has it Charlotte was strangled… by her own jealous husband…"

Livvy was dumbfounded. She polished off the scone and slurped down the tea. Mickey did the same, except it was his second scone.

"Well, I think we better get out there and have a look. Thank you, Mary."

Livvy easily located the spot where she had found the coins. She swung her detector over the area and the signal was stronger than ever, despite last time having retrieved all the metal she could find. Mickey did the shovelling, while Livvy used the pin pointer.

"Dig deeper, Mickey!" she commanded. Livvy was in a trance, she was wild. Every time they shovelled out the earth, the pin pointer screamed stronger than ever before, but there was no metal to be found. Livvy turned white. The peculiar feeling was coming over her again, and this time she could hear the haunting sound of a galloping horse, getting louder and louder, closer and closer.

"*Deeper*, Mickey! *Dig deeper*!" she screamed with urgency as the skies turned dark and the rain began to fall. Nausea swept over Livvy with a force stronger than ever before. She collapsed in a heap by the side of the hole, depleted of all energy. Mickey leant to her side.

"Liv! Liv, you ok?"

"Yes, I'll be ok, but you need to – dig – dig…"

"Yes, I know, *dig deeper*!"

The horse brayed. It was a ghostly bray that seemed to echo through the two dimensions with determination and a distinct degree of pain.

"*Did you hear that, Mickey*?"

He looked at Livvy, "No*, but do you* see *that*?" he said, pointing down into the very bottom of the hole (which was by now a good four feet deep). Livvy crawled to the edge of the crater, barely being able to drag her own body weight. She peered down, and as she did, she found she could finally breathe again. She let out a huge gasp, followed by another, and another, until her eyes were able to focus on what Mickey was trying to show her.

"*Bones…*" she gulped.

❧

From that day on, Livvy never experienced the shortness of breath again. Whilst she took a short break from metal detecting, it was not long before she was back out in the field, and her next find was a Victoria gold sovereign. She had found it so easily, and she couldn't help but wonder whether Charlotte had led her to it. Perhaps it had been a way to thank Livvy for uncovering her remains. Chris never did find out that Livvy hadn't rested up that day and took the credit that his sound advice had indeed been critical to her recovery. They continued to be a very happy couple and got engaged the following year. Livvy often handled the Victorian coins she had found, and although she never experienced anything harmful, from time to time she knew Charlotte was up to no good when the coins mysteriously turned up in random places, like on her knee when she was in the bathroom or under her pillow when she woke in the morning. Charlotte also had a confusing habit of taking out the scrapbooks from the bookshelves and leaving them open on random pages. It was a bit of a nuisance until one day certain photographs were forcefully ripped out from their decorative mounts, and Livvy felt certain it wasn't just typical 'Charlotte Tomfoolery.'

Livvy studied the photographs and then she realised that in each of them, the same young lady appeared among those caught in the picture. Livvy truly *did* have a connection with Charlotte, and it wasn't just random after all, and Livvy realised it had been her fate all along to discover

Charlotte's final resting place. What's more, she now had a face, and you know what? Charlotte had such an uncanny resemblance to Livvy; she was undoubtedly a relation. Livvy framed the best of the photos and displayed it in pride of place on the mantelpiece. From that day on, her love of history and her ability to connect with the paranormal only grew stronger, which made her metal detecting experiences certainly a lot more interesting that your average detectorist – as she was to find out not *everyone* was as willing to hand over their lost treasures as her dear Charlotte was that day in a field in Somerset, but that's a whole other story altogether!

BACK TO THE WOODS

What a wonderful feeling! I hadn't been back to Smith's Folly since, well, it's gotta be twenty years or more. Yet here I was once again, (a very different me, albeit), a 'grown up' me, yet I still felt that same sense of adventure that gripped me every time I entered this much beloved, and very special woodland.

Harry walked ahead of me. He always did. It was a bugbear of mine, like he was always on a mission to get to the next waymark, or to tick off the next place of interest. I only wanted to savour the experience – each snapped twig underfoot, the rustle of leaves and every squirrel scurrying around in the branches above. 'Go too quickly in life and you'll miss out on so much', my mother used to say, and it's something that really stuck with me, even to this day. I lost my mum ten years ago, which makes this philosophy even more poignant.

As we walked through the trees, we came across the open area where the Folly itself stood. It was looking a lot more dilapidated than I remembered from my childhood. The state of it made me feel sad, as I remembered how Sally used to claim she lived there – that girl always told tall tales, but she and I had a connection. We had spent countless hours playing in the woodlands, long after the other friends had been called back to their respective 'homes'.

"I can't believe it's been left to fall into such disrepair." I remarked to Harry, who had stopped for a rare moment to check out the building, which looked a lot spookier than it had when I was nine years old. The fact it was now scrawled with graffiti, and peppered something terrible with litter, didn't help at all with the ambience. It used to be such a magnificent, safe feeling place.

"Woah!" said Harry when he tilted his neck upwards from inside the folly. "You wouldn't catch me going up those steps. They're a death wish!" he shook his head disapprovingly. I mean, he was right – unsupported concrete steps spiralled around the inside walls of the structure, and they snaked all the way to the top of the tower. Some even looked like they were crumbling away.

"You'd have to be a *right* nutter to climb them!" he scoffed, whilst I remembered Sally and I doing just that… We wouldn't have a care in the world when we scampered up the staircase, nimble and sprightly in our size three pumps. Once we had reached the very top, we'd love to crunch up small, and peep out through the unglazed window, taking in all the beautiful countryside, and of course, among the greenery, we enjoyed the striking view of picturesque Tubbington Scrubby, often hearing the church bells from St Swithun's being carried over to us in the afternoon breeze. I bowed my head and avoided eye contact with Harry.

"*You didn't!*" he let out a gasp. "*Jess*, you didn't?"

"Erm, well…" I walked over to the first step and placed my foot on it, carefully rising to the second. My knees wobbled. Now that I was grown up, the thought of going up there again made me shudder and my newfound acrophobia crept in. "Well, I don't think I'll be making the ascent today, don't you worry!" I reassured Harry. I took a further glance upwards and felt sick. Just looking at the staircase (which had no banister, I might add) gave me palpitations. I was certainly a different person back then, but I always felt safe with Sally, and I could almost sense that she was up there now, waiting for me to join her. I remembered the sweet songs she used to sing. They were all new to me, but she enjoyed teaching me the tunes, and they were so beautiful and unique. Something disturbed the nesting birds, and an almighty racket ensued with squawking rooks and flapping wings. The outburst startled us both, and Harry urged us to carry on our walk deeper into the woods.

Our boots sunk into thick, sludgy mud on the narrower pathways – the ones that were heavily sheltered by the trees and didn't benefit from much sunlight. We had to be careful to navigate all the thick, gnarly tree roots that ran across the trail. They could be quite hazardous. Again, Harry took the lead, and I did my best to keep up, but I daydreamed about long summers that me and my holiday friends had once enjoyed there. Every year, the respective families would come to visit their relatives who lived in the Village. We'd pack up our bags with sandwiches and cake and be gone for the day. I recalled swimming in the river by the nearby weir – those days were hot and long, but our favourite thing to do was escape the searing sun and head into Smith's Folly woods and let our imaginations run wild. Sally definitely did that! Her imagination was wicked. She told stories of being trapped in the tower with no food or water until we rescued her from her tragic fate the first summer we all met. Hoping to write to each other over the winter months, we all exchanged addresses, but Sally insisted she couldn't give an address because she lived in the woods – she was a right hoot! Kirsty and Riley were my other best friends, but the years had gone by, and none of us had stayed in touch, which was an awful shame. I thought about what they might all be doing now.

Harry and I lived in London. I'd met him through my work at the publishing firm. He was a senior editor there and I, an editorial assistant and I also wrote fiction myself. We hit it off from the start, with our shared interests being a sound foundation for our relationship. London isn't for everyone, and I certainly missed my countryside routes, which is why I insisted that Harry and I took a break, and coming back to the county of Somerset in the south west of England was a 'no brainer' for me. I couldn't wait to share it all with Harry, who had grown up in Hertfordshire and never ventured this far south before.

Back to the Woods – Harry ploughed forward, leaving me in my own thoughts of Sally and our adventurous little posse of years gone by. Despite the fond memories, an uneasy feeling crept over me, and I started thinking about my mum. I missed her so much, and as I recounted old memories and fell more and more into a world of my own, I didn't realise how I was slipping further and further behind my much-loved Harry. Having been so caught up in my own thoughts; I didn't notice that I was now very much alone, and the more engrossed I became, the more the woodland seemed to wrap around me. My thoughts became wild and untamed. *Why* did my mum have to take that trip to Germany? *Why* did mum have to get on that particular 'Deutch Bahn' train? *Why* did mum fight the man off? *Why* didn't she just let him take her bag? *Why* did he have a knife? *Why* did she have to die? I stopped for a moment and came to understand I was quite lost. Harry was nowhere to be seen and I no longer recognised the part of the woodland I stood in. I opened my mouth to cry out for Harry, but in a flash, my face was met with a hot, sweaty, and foul-smelling palm that put a stop to my breathing altogether, rendering me stunned, and silent before realising I could still breathe out of my nose.

I froze! For a moment, everything was still, as if my captor was considering their next move. Then, without notice, I was dragged backwards violently, through twigs and branches which snagged my clothes, some of them scratching my forearms and hands. I closed my eyes tightly to avoid any of the sharp flying sticks. I couldn't scream, I couldn't do anything, and I just kept thinking *don't fight*. Mum fought and look what happened! So I let whoever, *whatever* it was, take me. I didn't resist in the slightest; I was a poor rabbit taken by a wolf, and for all intents and purposes – I played dead.

I must have passed out or been knocked-out by the brutal journey I had just taken, for when I came around, I was back in the tower. *The Tower*! Where I spent all those wonderful childhood days, feeling safe and secure with my friends, and I was back *there*, in the tower, about to be raped, or worse – murdered. My hands were now tied behind my back, and I crouched in the corner by the first steps of the spiral staircase. I trembled in fear of my life. He hadn't blindfolded me or anything, so I was certain he was going to kill me. There was no way I could cry for help with this repulsive gag that had been stuffed into my mouth. He was a robust monster, hideously overweight, and I'd say, in his late forties. The perpetrator was unshaven, sweaty, and stunk of something utterly indescribable. I panted, almost hyperventilating and vigorously shaking with anticipation for what I was sure was coming, but I still could not physically fight for my life, remembering how that did nothing for my mother in Germany. The monster brought his grotesque face down to meet mine, his mouth open just a fraction, with a revolting stream of drool dripping from the corner. The stench from his breath was enough to knock anyone out. As he leant into me, he smelled my skin, taking me all in, from my neck, up to my mouth and my own nose – he was an animal, and I was his prey.

The rooks were at it again, squawking and squealing with some devilish rumpus. I thought perhaps they were calling for help, but no one came. The monster precariously rose from his knees, and once standing, towered above me, uneasy on his two feet. He reached for his belt, and I saw how his belly was hanging over it. I gasped, this is it, he's going to rape me and then he will kill me. I thrashed from side to side, but he was so large, there was no escape. Surely Harry had noticed I was missing by now? He *must* be looking for me! I started to make grunting noises as I squirmed from side to side. There was no hope now... so I may as well try to draw attention to the tower. It was then that I heard it, a familiar voice, a song that I hadn't heard for years. It hit me – *it was Sally's song*. Ok, I was definitely hallucinating now... It was clear to me that I must be having some kind of near-death experience...

Beyond the hideous beast, a small light flickered. It caught my eye and distracted me from my abductor, who was now grinning from ear to ear, unbuttoning his jeans, jiggling his gruesome body with gluttony for what he was about to consume. I focussed on the light; it was comforting at a time like this, hypnotising almost, familiar too. I thought, how I must be preparing to leave my body and go to heaven. I wondered how he would actually end my life – would he stab me like what happened to my mum, or would he strangle me? I could certainly wait to find out... The light suddenly expanded and the song in my ears got louder and shriller and suddenly, the beast was no longer standing on his two feet, but he was hovering above me in the air with a panic-stricken look on his face. *What was going on*?! I couldn't wrap my head around the circumstances, this was insane, and just as I was coming to terms that my attacker was now floating in mid-air above me, he was dragged backwards with enormous force – although there wasn't anywhere to go, so he crashed in to the tower wall, and then back out to mid-air, and back again, and again, this seemed to go on for minutes. His bones broke every time he hit that wall. His screams were ferocious but merciless, as finally he was dropped in the centre of the small square floor space. Anyone would think he'd fallen from the top. His body was twisted and deformed, cracked and he was, most definitely, dead.

I was back in the woods. Harry was just a few feet in front. I gasped. It was as though I had just teleported there in a few seconds. I glanced at my arms, which were no longer peppered in scratches, and the filthy gag was nowhere to be seen.

"Harry! *Harry*!" I cried.

"What's up? You're keeping up with me pretty well today," he winked, "for a change!"

"Harry, *don't you ever leave me again*!"

"What are you talking about? You've been right behind me all the time!" he laughed, but I shook my head, wondering exactly what was going on. *Was I even alive*?

"Am I here, Harry? Am I *really* here?" I asked. Harry stopped and then walked the short distance back to me. He held both of my shoulders and looked into my eyes.

"Jess, what are you talking about?!" He was so perplexed, worried even.

"Oh, nothing …" I tried to piece everything together, but the puzzle wasn't an easy one, until… I took a quick look to my right and saw her. *Sally*. She was right there, walking alongside next to me! My dear old friend Sally, right there! *This was unbelievable*! She hadn't aged a day since I last saw her. I stopped and reached out to her, and she held my hand softly.

"I told you I lived in these woods," she whispered, before breaking out into one of her sweet melodies again. I'd never really been a 'believer', but that day changed everything for me, especially when Sally pointed to my other side, and there was my mother walking alongside me. They both accompanied me (in silence) until the moment Harry and I exited Smith's Folly woods at the roadside where our car was parked in the nearby lay by.

ൟ

Jess closed the laptop, and Harry breathed a sigh of relief.

"Are you finally giving that thing a rest for the night?" he winked.

"Oh Harry, don't complain – I'll never become a famous author if I don't *actually* write my book!"

"I know, but I just want to spend some time together with you – alone *without your laptop*!" he gave her a cheeky smile. He knew how important finishing her book of short stories was and would never dream of making a real fuss about her doing so. He moved over to where she was sitting at her desk and massaged her shoulders.

"That's nice…" she said with a dreamy voice.

"I was thinking… how about a weekend away?"

"Hmmm?"

"Did you say you used to holiday in Somerset?"

Jess laughed. "You want to go to *Tubbington Scrubby*?"

"Well, why not! You seem to rate it highly…?"

"Well – just as long as you don't walk off in front of me in Smith's Folly woods…" Thinking about her newly written story, that was *very* much based on *some* truths. She replied with a glint in her eye. "Have I ever told you about my friend, Sally?"

SPIN

I miss Rupert, that silly long-haired dachshund, what I would do to play with that dopey dog again. I'd make a deal with the devil to escape my unfulfilled adult life and be young once again, but flawless complexions, skinny thighs and pert breasts were simply unreachable, a thing of the past. Unless… unless I could get the motivation to keep up these insufferable spin classes at the gym. Alright, they won't take away the wrinkles, or hide my greys, but perhaps I could finally lose a few pounds off my well-rounded bottom before I fall hopelessly and miserably into my fifth decade?

I glance at the clock on the wall, and it glares at me disapprovingly as I consider skipping the indoor cycling class tonight. I've been at work all day, listening to other people and their problems – exhaustion is *not* the word. Demoralization, maybe? Whatever it was, it wasn't encouraging me to squeeze into my lycra shorts, tie up my trainers, and make my way to the foreboding health club. Pulling my heated throw around my torso, I think how I hadn't been feeling my best lately. I'm sure I'm coming down with something. Excuses, excuses. Come on Mellie, get your fat ass to that exercise class, you pathetic excuse for a human being, I scold myself. This is no good, I note the cat giving me evils from across the room, even

Samson thinks you're a waste of space.

Okay, okay, I pull myself up, change into my gym gear, fill my bottle with water, grab a sweat towel and dart out of the door and the cold air hits me like ice. Roll on warm summer days, I smile, thinking back to my younger times when summers would last a lifetime and back to a time when I was, well... – *happy*.

I arrive at the gym. It's not the fanciest of places. I can't afford one of those posh, exclusive gym memberships. A career as a customer service advisor doesn't really allow me to access a luxury fitness establishment, but this place does the job. It's really friendly too, not like those pretentious health clubs that cost two hundred pounds a month. I roll my eyes in disgust – but then, *who am I kidding? – if I could afford it, I would!* I'm the last to arrive before we kick off, and out of breath already, too. I awkwardly cough a little, before I clumsily set up the height of my handlebars and seat, and then fling my towel over the bike. Soon I'm good, and I jump on the bike, ready to feel the hellish burn – or maybe this evening, for the first time ever, I'd get that feeling that some of the other ladies talk about – euphoria? I doubt it! I think of my reward at the end of this nightmare, a nice glass of Pinot Grigio, and a lonely, empty house. I sigh and think about how I want to go back to my past even more, imagining playing catch with Rupert on my mother's lawn.

The beat starts, and the music is so *loud* that it feels like it's reverberating inside my bones. The room is darkened other than the geometric strip lighting around the edge, which reminds me of the best decade ever, of course – the eighties! I mentally prepare myself to be shouted at. The instructor is brutal, and she doesn't hold any punches, but it certainly motivates me to pedal as fast as I can. When we make the bike heavy, my thighs know it, I'm not sure which is more tortuous... fast or slow, light or weighty. What do you think? Both are a killer in my opinion.

We're climbing up a steep hill now. The pace of the music has slowed down somewhat, but it still has a strong beat and I'm standing up whilst pedalling with my hands clutching the middle part of the handlebars, in a sort of low crouched over position. I can hear some kind of clattering. It sounds like more work's being done at the gym. It sure needs it because the ceiling in the weights room leaks when it rains. Speaking of precipitation, beads of sweat are forming on my forehead and around my temples. The track blasting out is an upbeat version of Whitney Houston's 'So Emotional'. Since when did the 'Miss Trunchbull' of the gym instructors get such good taste in music? She usually plays a lot of that modern dance nonsense. I pushed through, using my body weight and those big old thigh muscles to power up the hill, only feeling more motivated when she screams, "*Add more*!" commanding us to increase the resistance. I touch the lever, moving it down only the tiniest bit.

My heart's beating real fast and I can feel my cheeks flushing as I work harder and harder, all the time getting closer to a skinnier, flatter me. "Keep it *going*!" the instructor yells. Like I'm going to let her win today. "All the way to the end – *as fast as you can*!" she hollers above Whitney, who is also doing a fantastic job of keeping me going. *Man, I love this song.* It takes me *right* back. I was about twelve when it was released, young, free, and careless, oh to be that way again, I'd sell my soul to turn the clocks back, to return to my best days. Only Samson, my beloved Burmese fur baby, would miss me. But why am I thinking of the impossible?

This is actually getting easier! I never thought it would, but my legs are going round and round, almost on their own. I take a big swig of water and wonder why I can still hear the clattering. A busy road runs alongside the studio, and despite the volume of the music, I can hear an ambulance's siren, or was it part of the soundtrack? Strange nonetheless, but it might be my ears playing up, I have suffered from tinnitus in the past, it must be that.

"And *spinnnnnnnnn*," she screams at us, "Keep it *going*!" I wipe my face in the towel, a little shocked at how fierce that woman was. I can do this! *I can*! I start thinking about my twin sister. I try to block Bella out as much as I can. Thinking about what she would be like if she was still alive is just too painful. We weren't identical, but we were certainly peas from the same pod. She had so much potential, so much zest for life. When the truck hit her, my life ended too. My desire to take pleasure in anything vanished. I was never interested in finding new hobbies or making friends. Academically, I failed, because I couldn't put the energy into anything to try to improve myself. Without my twin, I was nothing, so I let myself go. Forty years later, I'm trying to turn things around but I'm still on my own, and still as depressed as ever, childless, spouseless, friendless (apart from Samson, of course).

The tune changes, Bonnie Tyler's 'Holding out for a hero' comes on! Have I died and gone to heaven?! The tracks are insane today… right up my street, I can almost feel myself dancing as I pedal. A few concerned heads turn. Perhaps I need to wind it in a bit, but this is my era, ladies, and for once I'm *actually* enjoying the class… so take that! Yes! Yes! I'm truly feeling it, that strange euphoria that I thought would be impossible to experience. I'm feeling pretty good, and the bright lights are really helping me stay motivated today. Strangely, I begin to feel like the resistance isn't all that heavy anymore, despite the lever being nearly at ninety degrees. I wonder momentarily whether the machine is faulty, but quickly focus back on my body – I feel great! Greater than I've felt my whole life. What has come over me? I'm enjoying whatever it is, anyway, and suddenly thinking about Bella doesn't hurt anymore. In fact, I almost feel close to her right now. I can smell mum's perfume, the one that Bella used to spray on her neck. Those memories feel pretty intense at the best of times, but right now, I'm really feeling it.

Panting, I pedal on, and close my eyes whilst dreaming of my sister. When I open them, everything has changed. *What the flip is going on?* I'm no longer in a dark sweaty spin studio. Warm summer air is blowing over my face, and my hair is no longer thin and greying, instead it's long, dark, and flailing behind me as I whizz down 'Heatherbury Hill.' I look to my right, aghast, and there she is. Bella is right by my side. She looks at me and shouts out.

"*What!?* It looks like you've seen a ghost!"

"I'm fine!" I reassure her, grinning from ear to ear, "I'm just enjoying the ride!"

All is forgotten, and I'm back in 1984, dressed in my denim dungarees and cycling in the Devonshire countryside with my best friend, my twin sister – who *died* forty years ago. They say, be careful what you wish for, and I vaguely re-call wishing for something ever so strongly back in a world that I can't quite seem to touch. We pull over by a godcake, a kind of 'crossroad' with a triangle shaped raise grassy space, surrounded by the prettiest wildflowers. We chuck our bikes down and sit cross-legged on the verge.

"Shall we go to Nanny's?" Bella playfully asks as she picks a daisy and slices the delicate stem with her fingernail. "She might give us money to go to the penny sweet shop in the village?"

I feel like I've been punched in the stomach. There's something telling me we must not go to Nanny's today, however tempting those penny sweets are. I don't know what it is, but I'm getting the strongest sense ever that we must immediately cycle home to our mother and our dopey dachshund. Bella's pig tails make me smile. She and I love experimenting with new hairstyles, and Bella loves making daisy chains. She passes me the bracelet she has just made, and I wind it around my bicycle bell for safekeeping.

We spin around to head back to our home. A lengthy cycle ride lies ahead of us, and it's three pm already, but our mother never worries. We would be out all day when school was out, but she knew how well we always look after each other. Soon we're back and we are greeted by Rupert, who is so excited to see us. We play on the lawn, and mother brings us lemonade and cheese twists to snack on. Bella and I talk about what we want to do when we grow up. She wants to be an artist, and I want to teach. I want three kids, but Bella just wants a house of cats.

I'm starting to feel unwell, a little exhausted, no doubt from all the cycling. Mother thinks otherwise. She says I'm hot and coming down with a temperature. I must admit, I'm not feeling well enough for any tea tonight. Bella's gobbling down her Tuna Pasta Bake, but the fish smell makes me feel sick so I go to bed early, and mother gives me some medicine with the hope it will stall my fever.

∽∾

I slowly open my eyes. Where am I? I squint whilst trying to take in all the 'white'. There's a strong smell of disinfectant, and behind a glass door I can see the silhouettes of people scuttling around. I'm tucked into a bed, a little tighter than would usually be my preference, and by the side of my bed there's four people sitting around me.

"Mum?" I heard one of them gently whisper. "Auntie Bella! Mum's coming around – call the nurse!"

I look around at the faces surrounding me. Who *are* these people? I'm confused, and my head is pounding, but as I come around, I come to realise my three children, Lara, Bryony, and Gabi, are by my side, and of course, my absolute rock, my twin sister. Of course, but what on earth has happened and how did I come to be in… I look around again and see a plaque on the wall – how did I come to be in *Plymouth City hospital*?

"Mum," Gabi places her hand on mine, "Mum, how are you feeling?" *My sweet girl*, I think, but I don't have the energy to talk at the moment. I manage a weak smile. Things don't really make much sense, and I still feel a little mixed up.

"You had an accident at the gym, mum," Lara explains. "You fainted, mum, and then when you fell off the bike you were knocked out, and you've been in a coma ever since…" Lara squeezes my hand. "I think you need to be doing a gentler type of exercise from now on, mum," she giggles, but she's clearly concerned. My youngest, Bryony, looks genuinely scared. I want to take her in my arms, but moving is too difficult.

"Oh, Mellie," Bella says. "We've been dreadfully worried, and so have your students. Look at all the flowers and cards." She points to the table in the corner of the room, and I piece things together and remember my class of year six primary school children. At this point, everything is far too much for me. The nurse comes in and tells my family I need to be left alone to rest now. I close my eyes, thinking that I just cannot wait to be back home with my kids, and how lucky I am that I have Bella to look after me when I finally get out of this place. (She's a freelance artist and not tied to a nine till five.) I need to rest; I'll feel stronger soon. I know it.

※

The three girls and Bella made their way out of the hospital. They were eager to get back home as it was getting late, and everyone was exhausted, not to mention hungry. To make things easier, they decided not to make a detour to the 'Tesco Express' to grab ingredients to make Tuna Pasta Bake (A favourite of Bella's), but that they'd order takeaway as a special treat instead. It was touch and go for Mellie's recovery; a celebratory feast was certainly called for, for that reason alone.

They happily chattered together as they walked along the street to the bus stop. Bella reminisced about the times when she and Mellie spent the summers making daisy chains and riding their bikes in the Devonshire countryside. She very much enjoyed educating the girls about what it was like to be a child in the eighties. They were so engrossed in their conversations and so deep-down memory lane that they didn't pay nearly enough attention to their surroundings, on multiple occasions almost brushing shoulders, and narrowly missing bumping into other pedestrians altogether.

Bella didn't see the truck hurtling along the otherwise quiet road. By all accounts, the vehicle was going too fast, but if they had all been a little more observant, perhaps it could have been avoided. That said, if they had diverted to the Tesco Express, they'd have certainly been way behind the sleep deprived lorry driver, who also lost his life in the tragic collision. Mellie's three children were soon back at Plymouth City Hospital, but while they were huddled together in the waiting room, their Aunt Bella was pronounced dead.

※

In a nearby ward, I shot up in my bed.

"*Bella!*" I howl, as the heart monitor that's strapped to me starts to bleep. The next thing I know, a crew of alarmed nurses hurry in towards me. As I try to sit up and rip the sticky pads from my chest and arms, I cry out for Bella again. I tear around in the bed, trying to break free from the contraption which confines me. "What's happened to my sister?!" my unearthly wails rip through the hospital walls, and nobody is listening to me! They only want to pin me down to restrain me. Whatever strength I didn't have before has returned, and I fight as hard as I can to free myself. But it's four against one –I'm *never* going to win. The door opens and a tall man with thin brown spectacles makes an entrance. He's carrying a syringe. *What are they going to do to me*? I wriggle even more furiously, still screaming for Bella, but to no avail, for the scratchy needle pierces my skin, and the cool liquid, which must be some kind of sedation seeps into my veins, and once again, I'm in the darkened spin studio, wishing I could make a deal with the devil, I gulp, or had I already shaken his hand?

ABOUT THE AUTHOR

Tessy is a writer of poetry and fiction with a wide range of published works, spanning from rhymes inspired by the natural world to magical narrative poems set in fairytale kingdoms. Tessy is currently focusing on fiction with two full-length novels in the making, and a novelette called 'The Treehouse' available on Amazon already.

Tessy welcomes honest reviews and would be delighted if you had time to leave a few words about this collection of short stories. You can leave a comment on Amazon and/or Goodreads which would mean a lot to the author.

Printed in Great Britain
by Amazon